John Lee

Martin & James, or, the Reward of Integrity

A moral tale designed for the improvement of children

John Lee

Martin & James, or, the Reward of Integrity
A moral tale designed for the improvement of children

ISBN/EAN: 9783337011895

Printed in Europe, USA, Canada, Australia, Japan

Cover: Foto ©Andreas Hilbeck / pixelio.de

More available books at **www.hansebooks.com**

MARTIN & JAMES

OR THE

Reward of Integrity

A MORAL TALE

Designed for the

Improvement of Children

LONDON

Printed for & Sold by Wm. Darton & Co.
Gracechurch Street,
1791.

The PREFACE.

*T*O the publications which have already appeared for the use of
Children, the author begs to add the
following, being encouraged to hope
that, however numerous its imperfec-
tions, in other respects, the moral and
sentiments are unexceptionable. She
has, in this little piece, endeavoured to
illustrate that useful maxim, that " honesty is the best policy," and to prove
from example that those who are *adu-*

ated from mean and interested motives, frequently defeat their own purposes, and draw on a punishment where they sought a reward, while the generous and worthy, exclusive of their satisfaction, which must ever arise from a good action, cannot in the end fail of meeting a recompence.

The incidents of this little tale are in general simple, and the reflections such as the author presumed might naturally be supposed to arise from the situations in which they occur. With respect to the language it has been her aim neither to foar above the comprehenfion of thofe to whom it is addreffed, nor to defcend fo low as to vitiate their tafte. To conclude, fhould neither profit nor pleafure arife from the perufal of her tale, the author has at leaft the confolation to reflect, that no ill impreffion will through that channel be conveyed to the young reader.

MARTIN and JAMES,

OR THE

REWARD OF INTEGRITY.

A T a small village, in the Wes-
tern part of England, lived
a poor widow, who gained a livelihood by carding of wool. She
had one son, for whose sake she
chearfully underwent the fatigue
of working early and late. James,
for that was his name, was too
young to work; but he was a ve-

B

ry good boy. If by chance he
had a penny or a halfpenny given
him, a reward for his civility in
opening a gate, or conducting a
traveller through the village, in-
stead of spending it in cakes or
fruit, as children generally do, he
ran with it immediately to his mother, saying to himself, " my mam-
my must card a great deal of wool
before she can earn a penny to
buy us a loaf." Though it is natural for parents to love their children, their affection must propor-
tionably lessen or encrease as they
are unworthy or deserving of it :

This and numberless other in-
stances of affection which James
shewed toward his mother, rendered him so dear to her, that the
poor woman considered him as
the greatest blessing Heaven had
bestowed on her, and had nothing so much at heart as his interest.   As a proof of this, small
as her earnings were, she con-
trived by working early and late,
to save out of them sufficient
to send James to a day school;
where he was so attentive, that in
a short time, he was pronounced
by his master to be the best scho-

lar of his age, in the village.—
James endeavoured to repay
his mother's kindnefs by every
mark of dutiful attention ; of an
evening, when he returned from
fchool, inftead of going to play
with the children of the village,
he would read the fcriptures to her
while fhe was employed at work,

ever looking forward to the time when he fhould be able to work for her fupport, as the fummit of all his wifhes. But alas! this happy period was never to arrive—The poor woman was feized with a fever, which in lefs than a month put an end to her life. James was at this time between ten and eleven years old, an age, when he was capable of feeling the full extent of his lofs; for feveral days he wept almoft inceffantly, and refufed to take comfort; but time and proper reflection by degrees

abated his grief, and he began to
confider what courfe he had beft
purfue to obtain a livelihood; for
though he was univerfally beloved
among his neighbours, as well on
account of his own good behaviour, as of the refpect they bore
the memory of his mother, he was
fenfible that, in his mother, he
had loft the only friend to whom
he could reafonably look up for
a fubfiftence. He offered his fervice to feveral neighbouring far-
mers, but they all rejected him
on account of his youth, which
they alledged rendered him unfit

for bufinefs. They, however, employed him to drive the birds from the grain, an office, for which he received fo fmall a gratuity that had it not been for the humanity of his neighbours, who could not bear to fee fo good a boy in want, he muft have ftarved; yet fo cautious was James of intruding upon their kindnefs, that he many a day went with an empty ftomach, becaufe he would not make known to them his neceffities. In the fame village lived the fon of a poor cottager, who

had been a fchoolfellow of James's.
This youth, who was fourteen
years of age, had juft buried his
father, and found himfelf in pof-
feffion of four crowns; a fum
which the old man had by dint
of hard labour fcraped together.
Martin, for that was his name,
was always extremely felfifh and
undutiful; he thought the four
crowns amply compenfated for
the lofs of his father, and began
to confider in what manner to lay
the money out to the moft advantage.   He had been told, that
in London places were to be had,

where fervants lived like gentle-
folk; fuch a place Martin thought
would fuit his tafte better than to
follow the plough or to gather in
the harveft. With his four crowns,
therefore, he refolved to fet out
and try his fortune in London,
and by chance meeting with
James, communicated his inten-
tions to him, fetting forth the advantages which, he faid, muft in-
fallibly occur upon his arrival.
James liftened attentively to this
difcourfe, and naturally inclined
to rely upon the judgement of
others, could not forbear fighing,

that, for want of a little money
to bear the expences of his journey, he was deprived of fharing
thefe advantages.   His mind ran
fo much upon the fubject, that in
the evening, when he returned to
the dwelling of Ralph, an honeft
cottager, who, fince the death of
his mother, had afforded him a
fhelter, his difcourfe infenfibly
turned upon the intended journey
of his friend, and he could not at
the fame time forbear uttering a
wifh that fortune had put it in his
power to accompany him.   It
happened that evening, that feveral

neighbouring cottagers were af-
fembled at the hofpitable fire fide
of honeft Ralph.   As they all entertained great good will towards
James, they afked with one con-
fent, what advantages he could
expect from going to London?
James replied, that from what he
had been told, he fhould not fear
gaining employment of fome kind
or other, and that if he had money
to keep him upon his journey, he
fhould not hefitate to fet out immediately.   The honeft ruftics
feeing him fo much in earneft,
afked what fum he thought would

anfwer his purpofe? James pauf-
ed a moment, and then replied,
that he fhould not wifh for more
than three fhillings. Three fhillings feemed a very fmall fum to
perform a journey little fhort of
two hundred miles, but James at
prefent knew but little of travelling, and affirmed he could make
it do. In fhort, he faid fo much
on the fubject, and fet forth the
advantages of the journey in fuch
glowing colours, that the good
people, who had his welfare much
at heart, by contributing each his
mite, raifed the fum

and James with infinite joy and gratitude, by the affiftance of his good neighbours, fet out the next day with his friend Martin for London. The two lads travelled till late in the day, when growing extremely fatigued, and much in want of refrefhment, they made toward a tree, and were preparing to draw forth the contents of their wallets, when they perceived an old pedlar approach. Martin inftantly threw his wallet acrofs his fhoulder, and counfelled his companion to do the fame, faying,

C

that if the pedlar came to reſt near them, he would expeſt that they ſhould aſk him to partake of their repaſt ; " let us, ſaid he, go behind that clump of trees on the other ſide the road, and then he will not ſee us." " Why," ſaid James, keeping his ſeat, " ſhould we be ſo mean to hide ourſelves from the poor man ? he may not want our aſſiſtance, and if he does I am ſure he ſhall be welcome to a part of what I have. What ſhould I have done, Martin, if my neighbours had been ſo churliſh to me ?"

" I never think about other people," said Martin, " it is enough for me to take care of myfelf; though *you* are fo rich," continued he with a fneer, " that you can entertain travellers, I am not, fo I fhall leave you to your-felf." Saying this, Martin croffed to the other fide of the road, and fetting down among the trees, fo that he could not be feen, like a true churl, devoured his meal a-lone. James in the mean while took out a little brown loaf, and a piece of cheefe, with which his good neighbours had furnifhed his wallet, and was beginning to eat when the pedlar came up. "My little lad," faid he, "be fo kind as to help me to eafe my fhoulders of this box, for I have born it till I am weary." James, who was always ready to oblige, inftantly fprung upon his feet and gave the ftranger the affiftance he required. The old man then fat down to reft under the fame tree, and was civilly invited by James to partake of his homely fare. " I thank you, my good lad," faid the pedlar, " but we

will firſt ſee what my wallet af-
fords." Saying this, he drew
forth a large bag, and took out of
it ſome cold meat and bread,
with a bottle of excellent beer.
" Come my child," ſaid he, " eat
heartily of this, and if here be
not enough to ſatisfy us, we will
make an end with your bread
and cheeſe." James, who was a
very modeſt boy, at firſt refuſed;
but being warmly preſſed by the
honeſt pedlar, who would take
no denial, he fell to with a good
appetite. Their hunger being in

some measure satisfied, the pedlar took an opportunity of asking his young companion to what part of the country he was going; and being answered to London, expressed great surprise that he should attempt at his age, to take such a journey alone, and on foot.

James replied, that it was not long fince he parted with a companion, and that he expected him every moment to return; but he was too generous to difcover upon what account Martin and he had feparated. The pedlar, who was prepoffeffed in favour of James, expreffed a curiofity to know farther particulars concerning him; upon which James in a few words made him acquainted with his ftory, and the caufe of his fetting out upon fo long a journey. The old man fmiled when he underſtood, that the ſum with which his little friend deſigned to perform a journey of more than a hundred and ſixty miles, amounted to no more than three ſhillings, beſide a loaf of brown bread and a piece of cheeſe. "My little lad," ſaid he, when James had ended, "I fear you have heard a much better account of London then it deſerves; however, as you ſeem reſolved to try your fortune there, I will not diſcourage you. I am travelling the ſame road; if therefore, as your pocket is not very heavy, you incline to fave expences, and will fometimes carry my box, you fhall fare as I do, and we will jog on together till we are tired of each other's company."

James was delighted with this generous and unexpected offer, and expreffing his thanks in the warmeft terms, affured the Pedlar he thought himfelf happy in meeting with fuch a friend.

By this time Martin had made an end of his churlifh meal, and came up to the tree to rejoin his companion. The pedlar, who was an open hearted good natured man, filled out a horn cup of beer, and offering it, " had you come fooner, my lad," faid he, " you would have fared better,' for you fee we have juft made an end of a cold fhoulder of mutton; but here is a cup of excellent beer, and your companion can fupply you with bread and cheefe."

Martin thanked the pedlar, and taking the cup drank with as good grace as he was able, for he was not only extremely chagrined to think, that, through his over care he had dined upon bread and cheefe, when had he been leſs ſelfiſh, he might, like his companion, have fared ſo much better. But he was in great fear, leſt James had told the pedlar the real cauſe of his abſence. James, thinking to give his friend pleaſure, acquainted him with the pedlar's kind offer, not doubting but that he would rejoice in his good fortune; but Martin was by far too ſelfiſh. The happineſs of others never afforded him ſatisfaction; and in this inſtance, he was ready to cry with vexation, to think on the advantages he had loſt by his greedineſs.

For he was perfuaded, that had
the pedlar feen him, before he
engaged with James, he would
have preferred him to the office
of carrying his box, as being
ftronger, and more fit for the
purpofe.

Having repofed themfelves for
fome time beneath the tree, the
pedlar propofed that they fhould
continue their journey, and James
who was very mindful of his office, prepared to charge himfelf
with the box. The old man
feeing his intention prevented
him. " Stop, my good child,"

said he, laying his hand upon the box, " I am now rested, and as able to bear the burthen as yourself; when I am weary, I will call for your aſſiſtance." James however, could not be prevailed upon to relinquiſh the box; he begged he might carry it, alledging, that it would be a very unſeemly ſight for an old man to bend under ſuch a burden, and for two lads to walk at his ſide unladen. The honeſt pedlar at laſt yielded to the perſuaſions of his little friend, and ſuffered him to take the box

D

upon his back; after which, they all cheerfully fet forward.

James tripped lightly along with his load; and though the good-natured pedlar repeatedly offered to eafe him of it, fo anxious was he to exprefs his gratitude, that he conftantly refufed to refign the box; faying, that he was very well able to carry it. As for Martin, with the bafe view of fupplanting his friend, he made ufe of every art to infinuate himfelf into the efteem of the pedlar, and as a proof of his zeal and affection, which he thought could

not fail of pleasing, warmly op-
posed every attempt the good
man made to resume his load,
constantly alledging, that it would
fatigue him.

But all would not do, the pedlar who was a shrewd man, and
had seen a great deal of the
world, far from being won upon
by these extraordinary civilities,
conceived a distate to Martin,
whom he looked upon as solely
actuated by interest; for how
otherwise could he account for
his behaviour? Was it not strange

D 2

that he fhould pay *fuch unnecef-. fary* attention to a ftranger, and yet fuffer his old friend and companion James to toil on for fo many miles, without once offering to eafe him of his burden.

Toward evening they arrived at an inn, where it was refolved they fhould pafs the night; when Martin underftood that the pedlar defigned to fhare his bed with James, artfully drew him on one fide, and advifed him to let James fleep in one of the outhoufes, adding at the fame time, that he would pay him for half his bed, which would make the expence eafier for both. The honeft pedlar, who partly defpifed him for fo treacheroufly endeavouring to fupplant his friend, anfwered coolly, that he was already provided with a bedfellow, and advifed him to feek a bed elfewhere.

In the mean while, the pedlar called for bread and cheefe and fome ale, upon which, he and James made a cheerful fupper; as for Martin, though the generous pedlar invited him to par-

D 3

take with them, rather than en-
dure the pain of witneffing his
friend's happinefs, he left a good
fupper, and pretending extreme
wearinefs, retired to bed, where
he could unobferved indulge the
envy and rancour of his difpo-
fition.

James on the contrary went to
reft, as happy as a good fupper
and a good confcience could
make him; and with a heart
overflowing with gratitude, offer-
ed-up his thanks and praifes to
God, who, in the honeft pedlar

had raised him up so good a friend.

Early the next morning the two lads again set forward with the honest pedlar; James as he had done the preceding day carried the box, and to the great mortification of Martin, constant-ly fared with the owner; who was so pleased with his honesty and unaffected good humour, that he became every hour more attached to him. While James and his good friend endeavoured to divert the length of the way

by difcourfing upon different
fubjects, Martin walked fullenly
behind, wholly intent upon mif-
chief: it was death to him, to fee
poor James fo happy, and he refolved not to rife till he had found
fome means to interrupt his happinefs. Unluckily an opportunity offered: they had travelled
fome hours, and James ftill carried the box, when they turned
into a road, on one fide of which
was a deep ditch, more than half
full of mud. To the brink of
this ditch, as they walked, Martin infenfibly drew James, and

watching his opportunity when
the pedlar looked another way,
artfully gave him a shove and

plunged the unfortunate lad head-
long into the ditch.

The good old pedlar alarmed,
hastened to the assistance of his
little friend, and (with the help

of the treacherous Martin,) drew him all over mud out of the ditch. Luckily he received no hurt from the accident; but the poor boy was under great apprehenfion left the goods contained in the ped-lar's box were fpoiled. However, on this account he was foon eaf-ed; for the box being clofe fhut, few of the articles, upon exami-nation were found to be damag-ed; fo that a little fair water would foon repair them. This was a great comfort to James, and equally a difappointment to his treacherous friend; who was

in hopes the goods would have
been fpoiled, and the pedlar fo
incenfed againft James, that he
fhould with little difficulty have
fupplanted him. Having failed
in the fuccefs of his wicked
fcheme, it was his bufinefs now
to clear himfelf of all fufpicion of
being the perpetrator of it. He
attended James to a brook hard
by, and was very diligent in affift-
ing him to wafh the mud off his
clothes; during which, he* expreffed fo much concern for the
accident, that the poor lad, who
at firft fufpected and reproached

him with his treachery, thought
(as Martin pretended) that the
fhove which had knocked him into the ditch, was either the effect
of accident or given in fport.

James having cleanfed his per-
fon and the pedlar's wares, they
all three once more fet out amica-
bly together. James could not
fummon courage to afk for the
box, fearing from the late accident, that the pedlar might net
chufe to truft him with it in future;
but Martin, who was never diffi-
dent when he thought his intereft
concerned, warmly preffed his

fervices upon the pedlar; who, fhrewdly fufpecting that he was the caufe of the late difafter, abfolutely refufed to accept them, and perfifted in his refolution of carrying the box for the prefent himfelf, which he accordingly did, till feeing James look very difconfolate, and judging that his chagrine proceeded from the fear of not being reftored to his office, he very good-naturedly refigned it to his care.

Martin, however, could not yet give over the hope of fupplant-

E

ing the poor boy. He took an opportunity when James was at such a diftance that he could not hear him, to obferve to the pedlar, that it was very unfafe to truft his box with a boy, who, from his carelefsnefs was liable to the fame accident that had happened once, every time he fhould chance to pafs a ditch; befides, faid Martin, he is fo poor, that it is ten to one if he will not be tempted to pilfer fome of your goods.

Happily for poor James, thefe unjuft infinuations made no other

impreſſion on the honeſt pedlar
than ſuch as turned to the diſ-
grace of his enemy. He clearly
ſaw through Martin's drift in
ſtriving to villify the character of
his friend; and while he heartily
deſpiſed him for his baſeneſs, re-
doubled his kindneſs towards
James; but it was not long before the poor boy was deprived
of his good friend. The pedlar
was that ſame evening ſeized with
a complaint in his ſtomach which
proved mortal: having with difficulty reached a ſmall houſe of

entertainment about half a mile diftance, he immediately took to his bed, from whence he juftly prefaged he fhould never rife more.

James, who poffeffed the moft grateful and affectionate heart in the world, during two days which the pedlar lay ill, attended him with the fame diligence and tendernefs, as if he had been his father. Martin, though from a motive lefs difinterefted, was equally attentive; and refolved, however it might encroach upon his finances, to wait the event of the pedlar's ſickneſs. The poor man, who found himſelf every hour grow worſe, on the ſecond day after he was ſeized with the complaint, as James was ſitting by his bed-ſide, took him kindly by the hand, and in a faint voice ſaid, " James, I feel I am not ma-ny hours for this world; my life is going from me apace, and I ſhall ſhortly be borne to my long home.' James, you are good lad; had it pleaſed God to ſpare me, we ſhould not ſoon have parted; but his bleſſed will be done."

E 3

James could not fpeak for weeping, and the pedlar feeing him fo much affe&ed, rejoined: "Do not grieve my child, if you continue to be honeft and good, God will raife you up a friend when I am no more; and as for me, I truft I am going from a world of care and forrow, to a life of peace and joy."

James ftill wept, and in a broken voice, faid, he hoped that death was not fo nigh as he thought.

The pedlar fhook his head, and for fome minutes feemed buried in thought. Then looking earneſtly upon James, as if ſomething lay upon his mind which he wiſhed to communicate, thus began :

" My child, ſaid he, though my knowledge of you has been but of a ſhort date, I am perſuaded you are honeſt and upright. I have obſerved that you love God, and fear his diſpleaſure as the greateſt misfortune that can attend you on this ſide the grave. It is this opinion which makes me fix upon you in preference to others of maturer years, to execute a truſt, upon the performance of which my prefent peace of mind greatly depends.—It is now," continued the pedlar, "ten years fince the good Mayor of S——, in whofe fervice I fpent my youth, lent me forty crowns to furnifh this box. Since that time I have traverfed the country, and various fucceffes has attended me; upon the whole, God has profpered my endeavours. This faid he, taking a leathern purfe from a private pocket in his doublet, contains the forty crowns which are due to my honored mafter the mayor; I have faved them from the moderate profits of my wares, I thank my God they are not the fruit of fraud or unjuſt dealing.

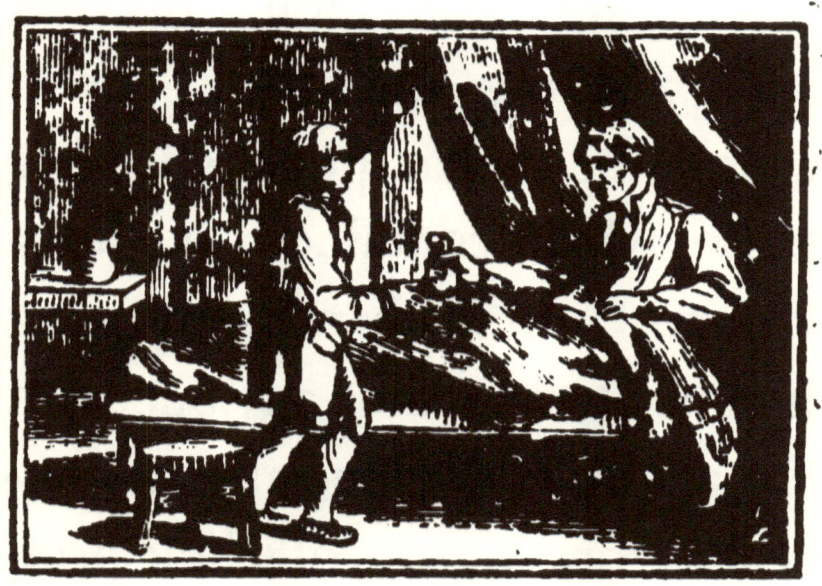

I reſign them, my child, into your care, and ſolemnly enjoin you, as you value the bleſſing of Heaven, which be aſſured as you perform

or neglect the truft, will punifh or reward you, when I am dead, to deliver them to the Mayor."

James folemnly promifed that nothing but death fhould prevent his executing the truft upon which the pedlar put the leather purfe, which contained the forty crowns, into his hands, enjoining him not to acquaint any one with the affair, and efpecially to conceal it from Martin, of whofe principles he entertained but an indifferent opinion.

The next morning the pedlar called for the mafter of the houfe, and after fatisfying him for the trouble, and all expences during his illnefs, he requefted him to be a witnefs that he bequeathed the contents of his box to the little lad who attended him, meaning James. He then began to talk of his diffolution as of a journey he was fhortly to go; and putting three pieces of money into the hands of the landlord, " As to my burial, faid he, this will defray the expences, and the care of it I leave to you as being my fellow chriftians."

The pedlar did not live long after; he expired before the next morning, and left James in great affliction for the lofs of fo good a friend. As for the legacy, he would not fuffer himfelf to think about it till the funeral of his good friend was over ; but having followed him to the grave, and paid all due refpeƈt to his remains, he took the key, and for the firft time fince the death of the pedlar unlocked the box, defigning, as the people of the houfe advifed him, to make a fale of the goods it contained, and afterwards to de-

termine in what manner to difpofe
of the money they produced. What
was the poor boy's confternation
when, inftead of the articles it formerly contained, he beheld the box
filled only with a heap of ftones!
This was an unexpected and fevere
difappointment; fometimes he was
inclined to fufpect that the people
of the houfe were acceffary to
the theft, and at others his fufpi-
cions fell upon Martin, who had
refufed to ftay till the burial of
the pedlar was over, and had left
the houfe early on the morning

F

after he died: the poor boy knew
not whom to accuſe, nor where to
apply for redreſs.   All his con-
ſolation was, that the forty crowns,
which ſince the pedlar had committed them to his care, he had
kept in his pocket, ſtill remained
in his poſſeſſion, as alſo the three
ſhillings with which he had been
furniſhed by his neighbours on
his firſt ſetting out, but of this
only a third remained when he
had payed for his board and lodging, ſince the death of the Pedlar;
and he ſet out to perform a journey of nearly ſixty miles with no

more than twelve-pence--in his
pocket; for as to the forty crowns,
the delivery of which was the
purport of his journey, he refolved, whatever might be his extremity, not to falfify his word,
with the pedlar, but faithfully, as
he had promifed, to deliver them
to the Mayor. James could not
forbear being much chagrined at
the treacherous trick which had
been played him, but he endeavoured to reconcile himfelf as
well as he was able to his misfortune, by reflecting that he could,

not be poorer for the lofs of that which he had never poffeffed. As his purfe was very low, he travelled all the firft day without any refrefhment but fuch as the blackberries and flows which he picked from the hedges afforded, and at night was content to fup upon a half-penny roll and fome fkim milk. The next day he purfued a courfe nearly as frugal, and having travelled till the fun had entirely difappeared, found himfelf in danger of being benighted, and overtaken by a violent ftorm, on an unfrequented heath. He preſſed forward as faſt as poſſible, and juſt ſheltered himſelf in a little farm houſe at ſome diſtance, as it began to pour violently with rain, and to thunder and lighten dreadfully. James thought he could not do better then bargain with the farmer to let him ſleep in one of his barns, and accordingly agreed to give him three-pence for his nights lodging. While they were talking, a poor ſailor who had loſt one leg, came to the gate and aſked the farmer to have compaſſion on a poor fel-

low who had fought many battles
in defence of old England, and
to give him a nights ſhelter in one
of his out-houſes. The farmer,
who was mercenary churl, and
thought the night being ſo bad,
he could make an advantage of
the poor man's neceſſity, replied,
" that if he could pay for ſleeping
in his barn he might ſtay, other-
wiſe he knew better than to har-
bour ſuch vagabonds."

- " Truely, ſaid the ſailor, I have
only four-pence to carry me fifty
miles, and if you will not for the
fake of charity afford me ſhelter,

I muſt ever be content with a wet ſkin." The farmer perſiſted in his reſolution, and the poor fellow was turning upon his heel to ſeek his fortune elſewhere, when James told the farmer that ſooner than ſee a poor fellow creature turned out in ſuch a dreadful night,

though he could ill afford it, he would pay the three-pence himfelf, which he accordingly did; and the poor man after expreffing his thanks in the moft grateful terms fhared the barn with his kind benefactor, who far from regreting the lofs of his fupper, which this generous action made him think it prudent to forego, enjoyed the moft pleafing reflections and grateful flumbers.

.. Early the next morning James again fet forward on his journey, but toward evening he grew fo fatigued, and fo faint from the little fuftenance he had taken for the three preceding days, that he fat down at the foot of a tree and. began ferioufly to reflect upon his fituation. " Alas, faid he, tears dropping from his eyes, what will become of me! I have yet many long miles to travel before I can deliver my truft to the Mayor, and many more before I reach London. My fhoes are already worn out, and my feet are fo bliftered that I can fcarcely ftand, and how fhall I ever be able to travel fo far without food. How happy would thefe forty crowns,

faid James, (taking the leathern
purfe out of his pocket) make me!
But then I have given my word to
reftore them to the Mayor, and yet
they would do me ten times the
fervice, for he is moft likely rol-
ling in plenty while I am ftarving
for want of food, and fo weary,
that I can fcarcely ftir from this
tree. Let me fee—with thefe forty crowns I could take the cot-
tage that my poor mother lived
in for fo many years, and I dare,
anfwer for a trifle could buy the
piece of land adjoining to it of
farmer Gofling.—Well, I could

then get honeſt Ralph of the mill
to aſſiſt me in cultivating it, and
the produce would perhaps make
me one of the richeſt cottagers of
our village.—No one, ſaid James,
purſuing his reflections, knows
that I have theſe forty crowns—
the pedlar is dead, and as to the
Mayor, he will never think of
enquiring after him, and if he
ſhould, nobody will be able to
tell him that I have the crowns.
Well, I am almoſt tempted to
take them.—(Here James pauſed
for ſome minutes, then reſuming
his reflections)—But after all, ſaid

he, would thefe forty crowns
make me happy after I have
broke my faith with the pedlar,
and committed a difhoneft action? No, though I could hide
my crime from all the world, I
could not from God; it would be
known to him, and he would un-
doubtedly punifh it.   It is true, I
am in greater want of this money
than the Mayor, but that will not
excufe me for taking what is not
my own; and yet thefe forty
crowns, faid he, looking at them,
are very tempting—What will
become of me after I have de-

'livered them to the Mayor—as to London, I fhall never reach it, and if I do, notwithftanding all that Martin has heard, places-may not be lefs difficult to gain there, at leaft for a poor friendlefs boy like me, than elfewhere—What will become of me? Should I attempt to return, it is as far to go back as forward, and how can I look my good neighbours in the face, when I have profited fo ill by their bounty?—But after all, faid he, what can befall me fo dreadful as the difpleafure of

G

God!—I·will look at thefe forty crowns no longer—I am fure money muſt be very dangerous to put fuch wicked thoughts in ones head—I will truſt in God, and endeavour to purfue my way to the Mayor---Whatever happens I ſhall be much eaſier when thefe crowns are out of my poſſeſſion."

Saying this, he rofe and made the beſt of his way to the next village, where with the few halfpence that remained, he procured himſelf a lodging for the night, and fome neceſſary refreſhment.

James was now quite pennyleſs, and had ſtill many miles to go; the goodneſs of his cauſe, however, ſupported his ſpirits, and he roſe early the next morning to purſue his journey.   Worn out at length with fatigue, and almoſt famiſhing with hunger, he was ſometimes tempted, for a moment, to take a ſmall part of the forty crowns, and tell the Mayor, that what remained was all the pedlar had committed to his charge; but when again he reflected that in doing this he ſhould add a falſehood to the crime of

dishonesty and breach of faith, he
resolved rather to perish than be
guilty of either.

While James made these reflections, a carriage with two foot-
men behind it approached.—The
poor boy, who notwithstanding
his fatigue, still retained his usual
alacrity to oblige, without thinking
what was to follow, ran and open-
ed a gate which a carriage was
to pass through, when a young
lady in the coach, who had ob-
served him, threw him a six-
pence.

James at firſt could hardly believe
his eyes, he picked it up with
tranſport, for in his preſent extremity it ſeemed like manna ſent
from heaven ; reanimated by this
unexpected ſupply he haſtened to
the next village, where he pro-

cured fome refreſhment, and to complete his good fortune, a comfortable night's lodging in the barn of an hoſpitable farmer.

Next morning he again proceeded on his journey, in excellent ſpirits, reſolving, as he walked, never more to diſtruſt the goodneſs of God, who in his greateſt extremity had ſent him relief. He travelled all that day and part of the next, and was beginning to grow extremely faint and weary, when a voice called to him out of a little cart that was paſſing. James looked up and perceived

it to be the poor sailor for whom
he had so charitably purchased a
lodging in the barn. The poor
fellow expressed great joy to meet
his little benefactor, and perceiv-
ing that he was extremely weary,
jumpt out of the cart, and begged
the driver would suffer that little
boy, meaning James, to supply
his place, at the same time telling
him of the service he had rendered him; the driver, who was e-
qually pleased with the generosity of James and the gratitude
of the sailor, consented to take
them both into the cart, and they

all fet off together. On their way
the failor informed James, that
when they laft parted, he was going fifty miles the contrary way
in purfuit of an old captain under
whom he formerly ferved, to pro-
cure a recommendation to Green-
wich Hofpital*, but that on his
way, he had learned his old com-
mander had removed his refidence
to another part of the country, to
which he was now going. The
failor faid, further, that being on
his way, the honeft driver in com-

The place where difabled feamen of the Britifh
Navy are taken care of.

paſſion to his infirmities had offered to give him a lift as far as
he went in his cart, and he added,
that he thought himſelf doubly
obliged to him for the ſame ſervice to his little friend.—Nor was
this all, the poor fellow's purſe
had been recruited ſince he left
James, and he poſitively inſiſted
upon dividing it with him. "Well,
thought James, a good turn is never loſt, I aſſiſted this poor ſailor
in his neceſſity, and at a time when
I leaſt expected it, he has rendered me a ſervice far greater." Luckily for James, the driver was go-

ing within a mile of the town where the Mayor lived, for he was fo completely worn out with he fatigue he had undergone, that this laſt twenty miles feemed more formidable than all that he had travelled before. The hour of parting being arrived, James, after expreſſing his hearty thanks to the driver, and the grateful failor, took a friendly leave of them, and proceeded to the town where the Mayor lived. Having enquired out the houfe, and with difficulty obtained admittance, on account of the fhabbynefs of his

appearance, thro' extreme pover-
ty, he produced the leathern purſe

which contained the forty crowns,
and delivered them, in the name
of the pedlar, to the Mayor. The
Mayor, who during ten years had
heard no tidings of the pedlar,
enquired kindly after his old do-

meſtic, and aſked James whether he was related to him. James replied that he was not; and modeſtly informed the Mayor of the manner in which he became acquainted with the pedlar, of his death, and the charge which he had in his dying hours given him to deliver the forty crowns to the owner.

The Mayor praiſed the honeſty of the Pedlar; but much more did he admire and applaud the integrity of poor James. It was with difficulty he concealed his admiration, when he reflected that a poor unlettered boy, reduced to the extremities of want, fhould nobly preferve his integrity, and withftand fo powerful a temptation; however, he did not think it neceffary at prefent to difcover all he felt upon this occafion. When James ended his account, he afked him coolly whether either of his parents were alive? James fighed, and replied that he had neither parents nor friends. No, faid the Mayor, that is hard indeed for fo good a boy.

H

At this inſtant news was brought that two countrymen who had taken up a youth on ſuſpicion of committing a robbery, waited in the hall for audience. The Mayor ordered them to be admitted; but what was the horror and aſtoniſhment of James when, in the culprit, he diſcovered his old friend and treacherous companion Martin.

One of the countrymen depoſed, that having obſerved a variety of articles in the youth's poſſeſſion, which he had a few months before ſeen in the box of an honeſt Pedlar who lodged at his houſe, and judging from the appearance of the lad that he could not have purchaſed them, he was induced to queſtion him on the ſubject; and from his confuſion and vague replies was perſuaded he had not come honeſtly by the goods, on which account he had brought him before his honor.

The Mayor, whom James had juſt informed of the legacy which the Pedlar had left him, and of the manner in which he had loſt

it, was perfuaded, this was the
very youth who had robbed him ;
prepoffeffed with this idea, he immediately called James, who remained almoft petrified with fur-
prife and horror in one corner of
the room, to confront the accufed.
James advanced reluctantly, but
Martin no fooner obferved him,
than thinking it in vain to diffem-
ble, he fell upon his knees before
the Mayor, and confeffed that
while James flept he had carried
off the articles contained in the
Pedlar's box, and to prevent an
early difcovery, fubftituted ftones

in their ftead.—James was afto-
nifhed at the treachery of his old
comrade; and the Mayor having
made fome obfervations on his
bafenefs, as a contraft to it, related
to all prefent the noble conduct of
James, to whom turning, *" You
refufed the forty crowns, faid he,
at the expence of your integrity,
now my noble boy receive them as
the reward of it."* Saying this, he
put the leathern purfe, containing
the forty crowns, into James's
hand, who, in a tranfport of joy
and gratitude, threw himfelf at

the feet of the Mayor, and could only exprefs his acknowledgments in tears and broken accents. The good Mayor kindly raifed him, and affured James that this was but a prelude to what he intended farther in his favor—" You fay, continued he, that you have neither parents nor friends; your virtue, my honeft lad, has in me, gained you both, for from this moment I mean to take you under my protection. But while I am mindful, faid the Mayor, to reward virtue, let me not forget that guilt remains unpunifhed."

Saying this, he ordered Martin to be feized and conveyed to prifon, there to await the punifhment of his crime; but James, whofe prefent happinefs did not make him unmindful of the wretchednefs of his old companion, threw himfelf at the feet of the Mayor, in the greateft agitation, and with tears and fighs entreated him to pardon his unhappy friend. The Mayor at firft feemed inflexible, but at length overcome by the diftrefs of James, yielded to his entreaties. " Go, faid he, to Martin, at the requeft of your friend,

I remit your punishment to God, and leave you to the stings of your own conscience—Go—and may you from your own disgrace, and the example of your honest friend, draw this useful lesson, that although guilt may flourish for a time, virtue and honesty are the most certain roads to happiness and honor."—Having said this he dismissed Martin overwhelmed with shame and disgrace. James through the generosity of the Mayor and his own diligence, obtained a liberal education, and the secretary of his patron dying, in

a few years he was thought capable of fupplying his place, which
he did with fo much honor and
integrity, that he gained the efteem and approbation of all, and
more efpecially of his generous
patron; who during his life, load-
ed him with favors, and at his
death left him a confiderable legacy, with which he purchafed a
little eftate, about a mile from his
native village, upon which he
lived happily to the end of his
days.

T H E

THE
AUTHOR
TO THE
READERS.

My little friends,

I Truſt by this time you have
peruſed my book, and have
not found the adventures of
MARTIN and JAMES deſtitute
of entertainment; I aſſure you,

it was my defign to amufe, as
well as morally to inftruct you;
if, therefore, I have failed, it is
rather owing to my want of abi-
lity than want of inclination.
With refpect to the moral, it is
fo obvious, that unlefs I fufpected you of great inattention,
which I have no reafon to do, I
fhould think it unneceffary to
point it out. I cannot, however,
before I lay down my pen, forbear recommending little James
(who I am perfuaded you admire
as much as you defpife his treacherous companion Martin) as

an example worthy your imitation ; when I call to mind his *modcfty*, his *patience*, his *humanity*, and above all his *integrity*, and *regard to his word*, I think I cannot prefent you with a more deferving model, You will, perhaps, tell me that, " As it is improbable you fhould ever be placed in the fame fituations in which he was, it is of little confequence whether or not you cultivate the virtues which rendered his character fo eftimable, and in the end raifed him to a fituation

I

far above his moft fanguine ex-
pectations." I agree with you
that it is improbable, you fhould
be placed *precifely in the fame
fituations*; but it is far more un-
likely that you fhould pafs thro'
life without being called upon to
exercife (though not exactly in
the fame manner) the virtues of
Patience, Modefty, Humanity,
and Integrity. On the contrary,
there is not a day paffes, in which
all or fome of thefe are not called
into action; your temptations
may indeed, be lefs powerful,
but then you will be the more

inexcufeable if you yield to them. Our Virtues as well as our Vices gather ftrength by habits ; accuftom yourfelf therefore to a ftrict examination of your actions, and endeavour to render them fuch as will be acceptable to God, and entitle you to the efteem of all good men.

Let Truth on all thy actions wait,
In profp'rous, or in low eftate ;
Revere thy fov'reign Lord on
   high,
Nor tempt his anger with a lye.

Let Envy ne'er thy breaſt inflame,
Nor ſeek to wound another's
    fame;
Bear with the failings of thy
    friend,
Be ſilent when you can't com-
    mend.

When naked, cold, diſtreſs'd and
    poor,
The wretched ſeek thy ſhelt'ring
    door;
Ah haſte to ſtill affliction's ſigh
To wipe the tear from ſorrows
    eye.

Let pride, and anger have no
    part,
Nor malice in thy youthful heart;
But *Virtue* all thy actions sway,
The leading star that points thy
    way.

F I N I S.

Sold by W. DARTON and Co.

Maps of England and Wales, neatly diſſected, 7s. 6d.

Ditto   ditto, on a leſs ſcale, 5s.

The ſeveral Stages of a Man's Life, from the cradle to the coffin, price 3s. 6d.

Diſſected Emblems of the Natural and Regenerate Man, calculated to promote a love for virtue, and an hatred to vice.

The Hiſtory of Joſeph and his Brethren, a diſſected puzzle, price 2s. 6d.

The Infant's Tutor, and the Inhabitants of the World, alphabetically arranged, and neatly diſſected, price 3s. 6d. each.

The School-Miſtreſs, neatly diſſected, for teaching the rudiments of learning, 2s. 6d.

The Farm-Yard, a diſſected puzzle, price 1s. 6d.

The Old Man, his Son, and their Aſs, who ſtrove to pleaſe every body, and pleaſed nobody, price 1s. 6d.

Rural Felicity, or the Pleaſures of a Country Life, neatly diſſected, price 1s. 6d.

The Tea-Table——Blindman's Buff, &c. &c. Price 1s. 6d. each, with a great variety of other articles neatly diſſected.

www.ingramcontent.com/pod-product-compliance
Lightning Source LLC
Chambersburg PA
CBHW032203010726
47493CB00008BA/2803